When Daddy Comes Home

Story by Linda Wagner Tyler

Pictures by Susan Davis

Puffin Books

PUFFIN BOOKS

Published by the Penguin Group
Viking Penguin Inc., 40 West 23rd Street, New York, New York 10010, U.S.A.
Penguin Books Ltd, 27 Wrights Lane, London W8 5TZ England
Penguin Books Australia Ltd, Ringwood, Victoria, Australia
Penguin Books Canada Ltd, 2801 John Street, Markham, Ontario, Canada L3R 1B4
Penguin Books (N.Z.) Ltd, 182-190 Wairau Road, Auckland 10, New Zealand

Penguin Books Ltd, Registered Offices: Harmondsworth, Middlesex, England

First published in the United States of America by Viking Penguin Inc, 1986
Published in Picture Puffins 1988
1 3 5 7 9 10 8 6 4 2
Text copyright © Linda Wagner Tyler, 1986
Illustrations copyright © Susan Davis, 1986
All rights reserved
Printed in Japan by Dai Nippon Printing Co. Ltd
Set in Souvenir Light

Library of Congress Cataloging in Publication Data
Tyler, Linda Wagner.
When daddy comes home/story by Linda Wagner Tyler; pictures by
Susan Davis.
p. cm.
Summary: A young hippo is delighted when his father, who doesn't
usually get home until his son is asleep, decides to set aside
special evenings for the two of them to work together on special
projects.
ISBN 0-14-050615-2
[1. Fathers and sons—Fiction.   2. Hippopotamus—Fiction.]
I. Davis, Susan, 1948-   ill.   II. Title.   PZ7.T94Wh 1988   [E]—dc19   88-11709

For my husband Patrick and our children Silas and Landry with special thanks for this story. And to Lynne Perri. — L.W.T.

For my Dad with love. — S.D.

My Dad comes home every night after I am asleep.

That's because he writes a story every day
for the morning newspaper.

He has to wait while someone called an Editor
reads it.

The story must be ready at 8 o'clock.

My bedtime.

My friend Tucky is lucky. His Dad comes home
every night at 6 and they read and talk together.

I asked Mom if I could stay up until Dad came home
so we could do things together, too.

She said not every night, but we could plan
to have special evenings.

Dad promised to come home at 7 o'clock
the very next night.

He said we would work on an exciting project.

And he told me to be sure to take my bath
and brush my teeth before he got home.

That night I was so excited I ate my dinner
very fast.

I put out my clothes for the morning in case
we stayed up late.

When Dad came home, he was carrying a
crystal radio kit.

He explained how it picks up invisible sound waves.

We worked very hard to put it together.

I told Dad about my day in school.

Dad talked about the City Hall story he is writing.

When we were finished we taped a green wire
to the window.

I listened to the sound waves coming through.

On the way up to bed, I said to Dad,

"Thanks for the radio," and gave him a hug.

Dad said, "I can't wait for the next project."

We listened to the weather report.

"The forecast for tomorrow is sunny and warm."

The next day Tucky wanted to see the radio
Dad and I built.

He listened to the sports report.

I showed him the instructions. "Wow!" Tucky said.
"I wish *my* Dad knew how to make things like this."

"But Tucky," I said, "your Dad tells great stories—
like the one about Paul Revere."

I guess all Dads are good at different things.

And it's fun for us…

to share them.